The Mystery of the Gingerbread House

THREE COUSINS DETECTIVE CLUB®

9610

The Mystery of the Gingerbread House

Elspeth Campbell Murphy
Illustrated by Joe Nordstrom

BETHANY HOUSE PUBLISHERS
MINNEAPOLIS, MINNESOTA 55438

The Mystery of the Gingerbread House
Copyright © 1997
Elspeth Campbell Murphy

Cover and story illustrations by Joe Nordstrom

THREE COUSINS DETECTIVE CLUB® and TCDC® are
registered trademarks of Elspeth Campbell Murphy.

Scripture quotation is from the International Children's Bible.

Published by Bethany House Publishers
A Ministry of Bethany Fellowship, Inc.
11300 Hampshire Avenue South
Minneapolis, Minnesota 55438

Printed in the United States of America.

Library of Congress Cataloging-in-Publication Data

Murphy, Elspeth Campbell.
 The mystery of the gingerbread house / Elspeth Campbell
Murphy.
     p.   cm. (Three Cousins Detective Club ; 13)
 Summary: When an intruder sneaks into a Victorian house that
is being renovated and begins stripping off the wallpaper in the
parlor, the three cousins help the owner investigate.
     ISBN 1–55661–851–4
     [1. Cousins—Fiction. 2. Mystery and detective stories.]
I. Title. II. Series: Murphy, Elspeth Campbell. Three Cousins
Detective Club ; 13
PZ7.M95316Mybej   1996
[Fic]—dc21   96–45911
                                                             CIP
                                                             AC

ELSPETH CAMPBELL MURPHY has been a familiar name in Christian publishing for over fifteen years, with more than seventy-five books to her credit and sales reaching five million worldwide. She is the author of the best-selling series *David and I Talk to God* and *The Kids From Apple Street Church*, as well as the 1990 Gold Medallion winner *Do You See Me, God?* A graduate of Trinity College and Moody Bible Institute, Elspeth and her husband, Mike, make their home in Chicago, where she writes full time.

Contents

"A trustworthy messenger refreshes those who send him. He is like the coolness of snow in the summertime."

Proverbs 25:13

1

Gingerbread

Over the breakfast table, Sarah-Jane Cooper smiled brightly at her cousins Timothy Dawson and Titus McKay, who were visiting.

She said, "Today we're going to visit Jack and Jill at the gingerbread house."

Timothy and Titus each stopped with a forkful of pancake in midair and blinked at her.

Sarah-Jane had seen that look before. It meant: Our cousin has lost her mind.

She stared back at them. *"What?"*

"S-J," began Timothy. "Yesterday at breakfast you were going on about how cute bees are."

"Yes," said Titus. "And today you're saying stuff that makes me feel like I woke up in the middle of a fairy tale. And besides, don't you mean Hansel and Gretel?"

Now it was Sarah-Jane's turn to blink. "What on earth are you talking about?" she asked.

"The gingerbread house!" said Titus, as if he couldn't understand where all this confusion was coming from. "Jack and Jill went up the hill. Hansel and Gretel went to the gingerbread house."

"No, no, no!" cried Sarah-Jane. "I don't mean a real gingerbread house like in a fairy tale—even though fairy tales aren't real. I mean a real house. And the gingerbread on it is real, of course. But it's not made of real gingerbread."

Timothy and Titus looked at each other and then back at Sarah-Jane.

Titus said politely, "Thank you, S-J, for clearing that up."

Sarah-Jane took a deep breath and tried again. "*Gingerbread* is what you call the fancy decorations on a Victorian house. People used to put fancy decorations all over gingerbread—"

"Real gingerbread?" asked Timothy.

"Yes, real gingerbread," said Sarah-Jane.

"So when people put fancy decorations all over their houses, they called that 'gingerbread,' too."

"Got it," said Timothy.

But Titus was still frowning in a most puzzled way. He was not at his best first thing in the morning.

"I thought you said we were going to visit Jack and Jill."

"We are," said Sarah-Jane.

"Then who's Victoria?" asked Titus.

"*Queen* Victoria," said Sarah-Jane.

"A *queen*?" asked Titus. "What? Like in a fairy tale again?"

"NO!" exclaimed Sarah-Jane. "I mean the queen of England a hundred years ago. She was queen for a very long time. And all the stuff people liked back then is named after her. It's all called 'Victorian.' "

Finally Sarah-Jane could tell she had gotten through. After all, she knew a lot about this stuff. Her father was a builder. And her mother had a decorating business. They both loved old houses, so Sarah-Jane had picked up a lot from them.

Sarah-Jane loved old houses, too. She

thought they looked mysterious. Not mysterious in a spooky way—unless they were all rundown. More like mysterious in an interesting, storybook way. Even old houses that were all fixed up looked like they could have secrets hidden inside.

And Sarah-Jane loved mysteries. So did Timothy and Titus. In fact, the three cousins even had a detective club.

"So," said Timothy, interrupting her thoughts. "You actually *know* people named Jack and Jill?"

"Yes," said Sarah-Jane. "And they've heard every joke in the book. So please don't ask Jack how his 'crown' is."

"Got it," said Timothy.

"Crown? What crown?" asked Titus. "You mean Queen Victoria's crown?"

But this time he was only pretending to be groggy.

And Sarah-Jane knew it.

"Don't make me hurt you," she said.

2

Paint Job

*W*henever the cousins visited one another, they brought their bikes along. This made it easier to get around. After breakfast, the three of them got on their bikes to ride over to the gingerbread house.

The boys did this just for fun. It was fun for Sarah-Jane, too. But for her it was also business.

Sarah-Jane had a messenger job making deliveries for her mother. If something was small enough to fit in the basket of Sarah-Jane's bicycle, then she could save her mother a trip. Since this wasn't part of Sarah-Jane's regular housework, her mother paid her. And sometimes other people hired Sarah-Jane to

13

run errands for them, too. So it could get pretty busy.

Today Sarah-Jane was dropping off some wallpaper samples. And she was picking up something Jill had found that she wanted to show Sarah-Jane's parents. Jill hadn't said on the phone what it was. But she had sounded pretty excited about it.

"The house is just around this corner," Sarah-Jane told her cousins. Then suddenly she and Titus had to slam on their brakes to avoid crashing into Timothy. He had just stopped dead in his tracks at his first glimpse of the gingerbread house.

"Oops!" said Sarah-Jane. "I should have warned you guys about the paint job."

She said "guys," but she especially meant Timothy. Timothy loved art. And it sometimes seemed to Sarah-Jane that he saw colors and shapes in a special way.

Now he just stood there staring at the house. His mouth was open a little, as if he had never seen anything so amazing.

"Jill says people either love it or hate it. . . ." Sarah-Jane began to explain.

14

"Well, *I* love it!" declared Timothy. "I *love* it!"

Sarah-Jane gave a little sigh of relief mixed with pride. "I love it, too," she said. "And I'm glad you do, because my dad helped Jack and Jill pick out the colors and decide where they should go."

"Uncle Art did?" cried Timothy. "Neat-O!"

"EX-cellent!" agreed Titus.

Sarah-Jane beamed. "And it was so cool!

15

Because when Jack and my dad dug down through all the layers of old paint, they found the original colors. And the original colors were almost exactly the same as the new ones! So the way the house looks now is the way it looked a hundred years ago."

"How about that?" said Titus. "I thought old houses were always just plain white."

"That's what a lot of people think," said Sarah-Jane. "And some of the neighbors complained about the colors at first. But then Jill explained that this is the way the house is *supposed* to look. And now some other people have even started to copy Jack and Jill by painting their houses. Of course, it doesn't hurt that Jill is the mayor."

Timothy hadn't joined in this conversation. He was too busy talking to himself about how the colors went together, and how the paint job showed off the gingerbread.

Timothy parked his bike in front and went off to see the house from the side and the back.

Sarah-Jane and Titus parked their bikes and trotted after Timothy.

3

Disaster Area

*T*he painters were still at work. Timothy walked around in a daze looking up at them. Sarah-Jane and Titus could tell that he was dying to get hold of a paintbrush himself. They didn't think he would do anything dumb. But they kept an eye on him—just in case.

Sarah-Jane said, "Sometimes people fix up the whole inside of a house before they even *think* about painting the outside. But other times people decide to do the outside first. That's what Jack and Jill did."

"How come?" asked Titus.

Sarah-Jane thought about this for a minute. Then she said, "I think Jill wanted to set an example for the town—what with her being the mayor and everything. Jill says it's good for

17

business if a town has lots of visitors. And she says that visitors will come to see Fairfield if we fix up our beautiful Victorians. That's because a lot of places don't have any old buildings left. They all got torn down."

Titus said, "Fixing up old buildings is better than tearing them down. Because once they're gone, they're gone."

"That's what Jill says," said Sarah-Jane. "But it takes *a lot* of time and work. My dad is doing the more complicated repairs for Jack and Jill. But they're doing the so-called grunt work themselves to save money."

"I can't wait to see the inside," said Timothy.

"Well, um—" said Sarah-Jane. "Let's just say it 'needs work.' Jack and Jill are going to take it slow and just do one room at a time. They're starting with the living room. In the olden days it used to be called a parlor. Nowadays Jack and Jill call it their 'disaster area.' "

"Sounds lovely," said Titus.

"How bad could it be?" said Timothy.

"See for yourselves," said Sarah-Jane.

They had been walking around the outside

of the house as Sarah-Jane talked about the inside. Now they stood outside the parlor windows. The cousins stood on tiptoe and peeked in.

The light was dim inside, so it was hard to see much. But they could see someone working in the room. It was hard to tell if it was Jack or Jill. Whoever it was wore a baseball cap with the brim pulled down low. The person also wore a little white workman's mask that fit over the nose and mouth to keep the dust out.

Sarah-Jane tapped on the window and waved.

The person inside jumped, glanced toward the window, and slipped out through the door that led to the hallway.

The cousins looked at one another in surprise.

"That was a funny thing to do," said Titus.

"Funny ha-ha or funny weird?" asked Timothy.

But of course they all knew the answer to that.

It was funny weird.

4

A Squeaky Door

*T*he front door was blocked because of wet paint. So the cousins went around to the back and knocked on the screen door. "It's open," called Jill, coming to meet them with a friendly smile. The door opened with an awful squeak. "Oh, dear," said Jill. "It's on my list of things to do."

When Jill did business as the mayor, everyone called her 'Your Honor.' But when she was helping her husband, Jack, at the Fairfield Historical Museum, everyone called her Jill. The names Jack and Jill just went so well together, no one could resist saying them.

Before Sarah-Jane could properly introduce her cousins, Timothy blurted out, "I love your house!"

Jill laughed. "Well, thank you! We're getting there. Slowly but surely. The place is shabby. But it's well built, so at least it's not falling down around our ears. Jack and I are really interested in finding out about the history of the house."

The cousins glanced at one another. Jill certainly seemed to have gotten over her nervousness of a few minutes ago. Now she seemed completely relaxed.

And she had taken off her baseball cap and workman's mask.

Sarah-Jane formally introduced her cousins and gave Jill the wallpaper samples.

"Oh, these are gorgeous!" Jill cried. "Your mother certainly has good taste, Sarah-Jane. I won't be ready to put up new paper for a while. But having these samples will inspire me as I'm digging down through layers of old stuff."

Sarah-Jane said, "I'm sorry we scared you like that. We didn't mean to. I guess we shouldn't have tapped on the window when you were working so hard."

But Jill just looked confused. "Scared me? When? What are you talking about, Sarah-Jane?"

"A few minutes ago," said Sarah-Jane, feeling confused herself. "You were working in the parlor. And we were on the outside looking in. That was us you heard tapping on the window. We must have scared you, because you jumped about a mile in the air and left the room."

Jill just stared at Sarah-Jane. "Sweetie, what are you talking about? I've been upstairs doing paper work all morning. I haven't been in the 'disaster area' at all."

"Jack then?" asked Sarah-Jane, almost knowing what the answer would be before she asked.

Jill shook her head. "He went to the hardware store. And once he gets in there, he loses track of time. He hasn't been working in the parlor today. No one has."

"Well, *someone* was in there just a little while ago," said Sarah-Jane. "We saw him. Or her."

Timothy and Titus nodded vigorously.

Jill gave a worried little frown. She turned and led the way to the parlor. The three cousins followed closely behind.

"Wait here," Jill said softly. Slowly she turned the doorknob and pushed open the parlor door.

5

The Empty Room

*A*s the door swung open, the cousins stood on tiptoe to peek into the room from the hallway.

Across the room they could see the window where—just a little while ago—they had stood on tiptoe to peek into the room from outside.

Jill took a few careful steps into the parlor. She stood with her hands on her hips and looked all around. Then she motioned to the cousins that it was all right to come in.

Sarah-Jane, followed by Timothy and Titus, hurried into the room. Like Jill, they stood looking around them. There wasn't much to see.

The room was empty.

Sarah-Jane was afraid that Jill would say

they must have been imagining things.

Sarah-Jane hated when that happened.

She had a pretty vivid imagination. And anyone who knew her—even a little bit—knew that about her.

But Jill said, "Someone has been in here, all right."

Sarah-Jane looked at Jill in surprise. It was wonderful to be believed, of course, but there had to be a reason.

"Is anything missing?" she asked.

Not that there seemed to be anything worth taking in the "disaster area."

Jill shook her head. "No, but let me show you something." She led them to a nearby wall. Her next question was a bit of a surprise. "What do you know about removing old wallpaper?"

"Grunt work!" said Sarah-Jane, who had helped her mother a few times.

"The worst!" agreed Jill. "It's such a tedious job that I like to keep track of my progress. It makes me feel better. And I promised myself that when I got as far as the fireplace, I could buy a book I've been wanting—as a reward. Are you with me so far?"

The cousins nodded. It sounded like a sensible plan.

Jill pointed to a spot nearby them on the bumpy wall. Sarah-Jane knew that one good thing about wallpaper was that it could cover up a lot of marks and bumps.

When the cousins looked closer they could see that the spot was a pencil mark. More than a mark. It was writing. It gave the date and time of day. Farther along, Jill showed them another pencil mark. It was the same date, but a later time.

Jill explained. "Whenever I get some time to work in here, I mark when I start and when I stop. That gives me an idea of how long it's going to take to do the whole room. If I hadn't kept track of my work, I probably wouldn't have noticed something odd."

At the words "something odd," the cousins' ears perked up.

Jill pointed to her last stopping mark and to the fireplace, her goal. In between, a good bit of wallpaper had been stripped away.

"And I didn't do it," said Jill.

monday
7:30pm

6

Mysterious Intruder

"*L*et me get this straight," said Titus. "Are we saying that someone broke in here to *strip wallpaper?*"

Jill said, "He—or she—didn't have to 'break in.' The back door was unlocked so that the painters could get coffee from the kitchen or use the washroom."

"Do you think it was one of the painters in here?" asked Sarah-Jane. She didn't think so, since these were dependable guys her parents recommended all the time.

"I can't imagine what any of them would be doing in the parlor," said Jill. "Did you happen to notice how many painters were working outside?"

"Three," said Timothy promptly. Being

detectives, the cousins had trained themselves to notice little things like that.

"That's how many are here today," said Jill. "If they were all outside when you guys tapped on the window, then it couldn't have been one of them in the room."

Titus said, "So if the door was open, it's not exactly 'breaking and entering.' And if nothing was taken, it's not exactly 'burglary.' "

Jill nodded. "All of our valuable stuff is upstairs. We're actually living up there while we fix up the downstairs. We're using one of the spare bedrooms as a living room and another one as an office. So the TV, the stereo, the computer—they're all upstairs. I was working up there all morning. I would have heard if anyone came upstairs. But not if the person stayed downstairs."

Timothy said, "So it's not a burglary. And it's a pretty weird kind of vandalism."

At that they all looked around the "disaster area." And it was as if they were all thinking the same thing: How could a vandal possibly make the place look worse?

"OK," said Titus. "So he or she is not a burglar or a vandal. We'll just say it was a mysterious intruder who likes to strip wallpaper."

It was then that Sarah-Jane remembered another odd thing.

She said to Jill, "When we peeked in the window and I thought it was you, I thought you were working. But it wasn't stripping wallpaper. I thought you were . . . sweeping."

7

The T.C.D.C.

*T*hey all turned and looked at the broom, which was propped against the wall.

Someone had been sweeping, all right. But only a little bit of the floor. Just the part of the room from the hallway door to the fireplace.

Titus said, "The part of the room where the person was stripping wallpaper is clean. The rest of the floor is dusty."

Timothy said, "A mysterious intruder who sneaks into your house to clean it?" But he didn't sound as if he actually believed that.

Sarah-Jane had a sudden thought. "No," she said. "A mysterious intruder who wants to cover his tracks. Someone wanted to get rid of any telltale footprints in the dust."

"Wow!" said Jill. "You kids are really sharp!"

"We have to be," said Titus with a grin. "We're the T.C.D.C."

"What's a 'teesy-deesy'?" asked Jill.

"It's letters," explained Sarah-Jane. "Capital T. Capital C. Capital D. Capital C. It stands for the Three Cousins Detective Club."

Jill said, "Well, that sounds like exactly the kind of help I could use right now."

Jack came home from the hardware store just then, and Jill explained what had happened.

Jack suggested they double-check upstairs to make sure nothing was missing.

Jill told the cousins to come along, since she wanted to give them a tour of the house anyway. People who were working on a house always seemed to want to do that.

And the cousins, being detectives, wanted to look around.

The first thing Timothy noticed was a little pile of workmen's masks on the table outside the parlor door.

"We keep some extras handy," Jill explained. "You don't want to breathe in a lot of dust and dirt."

Timothy counted four. "Are any missing?" he asked.

Jill frowned, trying to remember. "I really don't know. Why do you ask? Oh, that's right—you said the person you saw in the parlor was wearing one."

"Pretty careful, wasn't he?" remarked Jack. "Sneaks into somebody's 'disaster area,' but is careful not to breathe the dirt in there."

"Yes . . ." said Timothy slowly. "But I was

also thinking . . . A baseball cap pulled down low . . . A workman's dust mask over your nose and mouth . . . Put it all together, and you've got a pretty good disguise."

8

An Unexpected Visitor

No one quite knew what to say to that. It was all so strange.

Jack and Jill led the way upstairs.

Sarah-Jane saw Timothy and Titus glance at each other. Sarah-Jane had been known to exaggerate from time to time. But saying the house "needed work"—that was an understatement.

The cousins were too polite to say anything. But Jack and Jill seemed to guess what they were thinking.

Jack said, "Sometimes we wonder what we've gotten ourselves into. But it will look great by the time we're done."

"How long will that take?" asked Titus. He couldn't keep the amazement out of his voice.

Jack laughed. "Probably the rest of our lives. But it's worth it to us to live in a little piece of history."

"Also—" said Jill. "We love the idea of saving the house. We don't even feel like owners exactly. More like caretakers. We feel that we're saving something lovely from the past as a kind of gift to people in the future."

Jack added, "It's the same reason people have museums. And, by the way, our little Fairfield Historical Museum is coming along nicely. People have been finding some wonderful things tucked away in old attics. And they've been very generous about donating them to the museum."

"My dad teaches history," Titus said.

And it turned out that Jack had met Titus's father at a history convention.

As they came downstairs, they were all busy talking about what a small world it was. So they were startled to see a woman standing in the kitchen by the back door.

The woman looked even more startled than they were. She gave a nervous little laugh and said, "Oh! There you are! I knocked, but you must not have heard me. So I just opened the door and came on in. I hope you don't mind."

"No, not at all," said Jill, but sounding a little surprised. To the cousins she said, "This is our neighbor, Mrs. Pruitt." And to Mrs. Pruitt she said, "What can I do for you?"

"Oh! Um—I just thought I'd stop by and see that old photograph you mentioned the other day at the office."

"Good timing," replied Jill. "I was just about to send it home with Sarah-Jane. I wanted Art and Sue Cooper to see it."

Jill went to get the photograph. And Jack set out sugar cookies and lemonade.

Mrs. Pruitt and the cousins sat down at the kitchen table.

It was all very nice.

Sarah-Jane didn't know why she felt something was wrong.

9

An Old-Time Photograph

*J*ill came back with the photograph, and they all crowded around to see it.

"That's your house!" Timothy said to Jack and Jill.

"That's *this* house!" agreed Titus. "The one we're sitting in right now."

"It's the gingerbread house when it was new!" said Sarah-Jane.

Mrs. Pruitt just looked at the picture and nodded.

"The photograph is in black-and-white, of course," said Jack. "They didn't have color film back then. But you can see from the different shadings that the house was painted in several different colors. And your dad, Sarah-Jane, did a really great job of planning where the colors should go. His plan was almost exactly the same as the original paint job. I thought he'd like to see this."

"Oh, I know he will," said Sarah-Jane. "He's always looking at pictures of old buildings. That's one reason he likes to go to the museum so much. So does my mother."

"Your parents have a real feel for what they're doing," said Jill.

"Yes," agreed Sarah-Jane. Then she added, "Thank you," because it was a compliment to her family.

Jack got out a big magnifying glass so that they could all look at the picture more closely. Being detectives, the cousins loved magnifying glasses.

In the picture they could clearly see the beautiful gingerbread carving all around the front porch.

They could also look up close at three children standing on the porch.

"Who are those kids?" asked Titus.

Jill said, "The original owner had a son and a daughter." She pointed to the teenage boy in

the picture. Sarah-Jane thought that he probably wouldn't have liked being called a kid.

"The names are written on the back," said
Jill. "The boy is Henry. And this is his sister,
Lucy, standing next to him." The girl she
pointed to was about the cousins' age. "And
the girl standing next to Lucy is Charlotte. She
was a friend of Lucy's, it says."

Sarah-Jane looked long and hard at the
faces of the long-ago children. Henry looked

bored, she thought. As if he didn't like being lumped together with the two mischievous girls beside him.

Mischievous. That's exactly how Lucy and Charlotte looked, thought Sarah-Jane. Those girls were up to something.

Sarah-Jane wished she could have been in on the secret with them. She had a feeling it had something to do with Henry.

Suddenly Sarah-Jane felt a little twinge of disappointment that she would never know what the secret was.

10

A Scrap of a Clue

"W here did you find the photograph?" asked Mrs. Pruitt.

"It fell out from behind some shelves when we moved them," Jill replied. "I expect we'll find all sorts of things when we really get going on this place. Lucy lived in the house for many, many years after she grew up. And it stood empty for a while. But you know what they say about old houses: 'If only these walls could talk.'"

"Yes. Well," said Mrs. Pruitt. "Thank you so much for the lemonade and cookies. I'm sorry I can't stay any longer. But I've been rushing here, there, and everywhere this morning. I had a couple of spare moments. So

I thought I'd pop in and see your lovely old photograph."

Jill walked her unexpected guest to the back door. The door opened with such a noisy squeak that Mrs. Pruitt jumped.

"Oh, dear!" said Jill. "I spend so much time apologizing for this door that it would be easier just to fix it. It's on my list of things to do."

After Mrs. Pruitt had gone, the cousins helped Jack and Jill clear the table and wash the dishes.

Then Jack went outside with lemonade and cookies for the painters.

And Jill went to take a telephone call.

So the cousins were alone in the kitchen.

Sarah-Jane was just wiping up the last of the cookie crumbs from the table when she spotted a scrap of something on the floor.

It was lying under a door that led to a little room off the kitchen. Actually, the room was more like a big closet. Jill had explained that this was an old-fashioned pantry, a place for storing extra food.

The little scrap looked like it was half in the pantry and half in the kitchen.

Since she was clearing up anyway, Sarah-Jane went to pick up the scrap. It was just a little bit of paper. But it looked oddly familiar. One side was kind of sticky. Sarah-Jane turned it over. There was a design on the other side.

She was holding a scrap of wallpaper from the parlor.

11

A Sticky Situation

Sarah-Jane realized she must have gasped, because her cousins came rushing over.

"What's the matter?" asked Timothy.

"What's that in your hand?" asked Titus.

Sarah-Jane held out the scrap of wallpaper.

"Isn't that from the parlor?" asked Timothy.

"Yes, it is," said Sarah-Jane. "So what's it doing in the kitchen?"

"It's kind of sticky," said Titus, thinking out loud. "So—maybe it got stuck to the bottom of one of our shoes when we were in the parlor. There were a lot of scraps of wallpaper in there."

As soon as he said this, all three of them automatically checked their shoes. But none of them had any wallpaper stuck there.

"But," said Titus, "maybe when we came in the kitchen, it got unstuck."

"That idea makes a lot of sense, Ti," said Sarah-Jane. "Except for one thing. None of us went near the pantry. And the scrap wasn't just *near* the pantry. It was partway *inside* the pantry. So how did it get there?"

"Jack or Jill?" asked Timothy.

"Maybe," said Sarah-Jane. "But when? They hadn't been in the parlor for a while. And then they were with us the whole time. I didn't see either one of them go in the pantry."

"It could have been there from before today," said Titus, still thinking out loud.

"True," said Sarah-Jane. "But you'd think they would have found the paper by now and picked it up. Their house is shabby, not dirty."

Jill came back in time to hear the tail end of this conversation, which made Sarah-Jane feel a little embarrassed. But Jill just thought it was funny and gave Sarah-Jane a little hug to say so.

But what wasn't funny was the question of how the wallpaper scrap had gotten into the pantry.

12

The Hiding Place

Sarah-Jane had a pretty good idea of how the scrap of wallpaper had gotten from the parlor to the kitchen pantry.

But before she could say anything, the back door squeaked open, and Jack came in.

He said, "You haven't seen a baseball cap around here, have you? One of the painters just told me he's missing his. He said he left it out back. But when he went to get it, it was gone."

Everyone looked around blankly the way people do when they have no idea where something is but when they want to be helpful. It was as if just by looking hard enough, the thing might pop out of thin air.

That's almost what happened.

Titus spotted the cap shoved down in the

narrow space between the garbage can and the back door.

"Well, I'll be!" cried Jack. "What's it doing down there?"

He pulled it out, and the cousins knew right away where they had seen it before. Pulled down low on the head of the mysterious intruder.

"Come here a minute," said Timothy. "I want to check something out."

He led them to the little table outside the parlor.

"Aha!" he said. "Just as I thought. Somebody used one of these masks and then put it back. Probably hoping no one would notice that it was ever gone. But I counted them before. First there were four. And now there are five."

"What's going on here?" said Jill.

"Well, first of all," said Sarah-Jane. "I think somebody needed to get into the parlor for whatever crazy reason. Maybe this person saw the painters going in and out and knew the back door was unlocked.

"Maybe this person even saw Jill working by the upstairs window and saw Jack drive off. If the painters were working on the other side of the house, the coast would be clear.

"But maybe this person saw the baseball cap out back and thought it wouldn't hurt to look like one of the painters—just in case.

"And it goes OK at first. This person comes in, puts on a workman's mask, and gets to work stripping wallpaper."

"Go figure," said Titus.

"I know," agreed Sarah-Jane. "I haven't been able to figure that part out yet."

"So, anyway, *we* come along and tap on the

window because we think it's Jill. And this person has to get out of there. But sneaking out of the house was not as easy as sneaking in. Maybe the intruder heard Jill coming downstairs or us coming to the door. I think the person hid in the pantry. I think that's how the wallpaper got there. It was on the intruder's shoe.

"And I think when we were on the tour, this person snuck out of the pantry, put the mask back on the table, and ditched the baseball cap between the garbage can and the door."

They were all quiet for a moment, thinking about this.

"Sounds good, S-J," said Titus. "But I have a question."

Sarah-Jane didn't mind. It was kind of a rule they had. Whenever one of them had a theory, the others were free to say what might be wrong with it—as long as they did it in a nice way.

"My question," said Titus, "is why ditch the baseball cap there? Why not just take it back outside and put it back where it belonged? It would be less suspicious that way."

Sarah-Jane had to agree. It was a good question.

"And I have a question, too," said Timothy. "How did this person get out without running into Mrs. Pruitt?"

And Sarah-Jane agreed that this was a good question, too.

At the back of her mind, she thought she knew the answer to both of them—almost.

13

Grunt Work

"*I*t seems to me," said Jill, "that the answer to all these questions lies somewhere in the parlor. Somewhere under the wallpaper."

"Don't tell me. Let me guess," said Sarah-Jane. "This means grunt work."

"I'm afraid so," said Jill. "I think the only answer is to get in there and see if we can figure out what this person was after."

Sarah-Jane had called it grunt work. But actually she was dying to help. So were Timothy and Titus. After all, a lot of detective work was grunt work. Digging around. Looking for answers. Asking questions.

Sarah-Jane went to call her parents to ask if she and Timothy and Titus could stay to help Jack and Jill.

It took a while—quite a while—to explain why they were begging to be allowed to strip wallpaper.

But when Sarah-Jane's parents heard how mysterious it all was, they decided to get in on it, too.

So, before long, the four grown-ups and the three kids were hard at work.

"Tell me again what we're looking for," said Sarah-Jane's father.

"We don't have the slightest idea," said Sarah-Jane cheerfully. "But we'll know it when we find it."

And in the end, it was Sarah-Jane who found it.

At first she thought it was just a bump on the wall. But as she pulled away the bottom layer of wallpaper, she knew she had found something.

It was a thin envelope.

Everyone came rushing over to see what Sarah-Jane had found. Then they took it out to the kitchen table, away from the dust and dirt.

It was a letter. Dated almost a hundred years ago.

"It's from Lucy and Charlotte!" cried Sarah-Jane, jumping ahead to the signatures. "The girls in the old-time picture!"

Jill got the photograph out again. And Sarah-Jane studied the mischievous faces. Yes, those girls had been up to something.

The letter said:

To Whom It May Concern:

Because we are not allowed to add our Letter-to-the-Future to the time capsule being prepared by the most unkind Henry Kimball and his mean-spirited friends, we are resolved to prepare our own. Lucy's question: Have any of your explorers yet found the North Pole? Charlotte's question: Have any of your inventors made a flying machine? P.S. We found this elegant paper in an old trunk in Lucy's attic, and we thought it most fitting for our Letter-to-the-Future.

Lucy Kimball and Charlotte Ryan

14

The Discovery

"*T*he letter is charming!" said Jill. "What fun to get a message from the past!" She paused. "But it still doesn't explain why our intruder was so desperate to get it. Or how the intruder even knew it was there."

Jack said, "The paper it's written on is certainly more than a hundred years old. And there's something written on the back."

Jack turned the letter over and examined the other side. Then he almost fell off his chair.

"What? What is it?" everyone asked.

"This is a very rare and important historical document," Jack said. "If it's the real thing, it's worth a small fortune. Not to mention the historical value to a museum. You hear about this kind of thing sometimes—papers of tre-

mendous value being shut away in a trunk somewhere. We will have to have some experts look at this, of course. But I think we have really found something!"

Sarah-Jane's mother said, "But again— how in the world did the intruder know this was hidden in your parlor?"

Jill said, "Believe me, if I knew who it was, I would get an answer to that!"

No one doubted she could do it. Jill was very nice. But she was also the mayor. And she could be one tough cookie when she needed to be.

"But we don't know who was prowling around here," said Jack.

Once again, Sarah-Jane had the feeling that she knew more than she thought she did.

Just then the back door opened with its awful squeak, and everyone jumped.

"Sorry to scare you!" It was one of the painters. "I just wanted to let you know that we're breaking for lunch now."

"OK—thanks!" said Jack.

He turned back to the people at the table. "What was I saying? Oh, yes—we'll probably never know who the intruder was."

"I know who it was," said Sarah-Jane.

Because—suddenly—she did.

15

Answers

*E*veryone turned to stare at her, waiting for an explanation.

"The door didn't squeak," said Sarah-Jane. "When we came downstairs after the tour, Mrs. Pruitt was just standing there by the back door. She didn't have time to get out before we saw her. So she just turned around and pretended that she had just come in. She said she knocked. Well, *maybe* we wouldn't have heard that. But we would certainly have heard the door squeak if she had just come in. But the door didn't squeak. I'm positive."

"Now that you mention it," said Jill, "so am I."

"So what are we saying?" asked Timothy. "That Mrs. Pruitt had time to put the mask back on the hallway table? But that she didn't have time to get outside with the baseball cap? That answers Ti's question about what the cap was doing stuffed down behind the garbage can."

"Yes," said Titus. "And it also answers Tim's question about how the intruder got out without running into Mrs. Pruitt. The intruder *was* Mrs. Pruitt."

"Excuse me," said Jill. "I have to make a phone call."

———

A little while later Jill came back with a firm but satisfied look on her face.

"I got the whole story," she announced. "It seems Mrs. Pruitt bought a box of old books at an estate sale. And among those books was a childhood journal written by Charlotte Ryan. In it, she tells about the 'time capsule' she and Lucy hid behind a piece of loose wallpaper, which they then pasted in place. She also described what was on the other side of the paper they used—although she had no idea how important it was.

"I imagine the girls might later have forgotten all about their letter. People are always forgetting where they've put time capsules. They turn up in some interesting places. Maybe one day we'll come across Henry's. And in the meantime, we will see that this valuable document ends up in the Fairfield Historical Museum. If Mrs. Pruitt had found it first, she would have sold it to a private collector for a great deal of money."

Sarah-Jane was glad about the document, of course. But she was actually more interested in Lucy and Charlotte and their message from the past. She had learned the secret.

As if reading her mind, her mother said, "Well, Sarah-Jane, you and your cousins got quite a bit done on your messenger job today!"

Jill said she couldn't agree more. And as a special thank-you, she gave Sarah-Jane the old-time photograph of Lucy and Charlotte (and mean old Henry) standing on the porch of the gingerbread house.

The End

Series for Young Readers*
From Bethany House Publishers

★ ★ ★

THE ADVENTURES OF CALLIE ANN
by Shannon Mason Leppard
Readers will giggle their way through the true-to-life escapades of Callie Ann Davies and her many North Carolina friends.

★ ★ ★

BACKPACK MYSTERIES
by Mary Carpenter Reid
This excitement-filled mystery series follows the mishaps and adventures of Steff and Paulie Larson as they strive to help often-eccentric relatives crack their toughest cases.

★ ★ ★

THE CUL-DE-SAC KIDS
by Beverly Lewis
Each story in this lighthearted series features the hilarious antics and predicaments of nine endearing boys and girls who live on Blossom Hill Lane.

★ ★ ★

RUBY SLIPPERS SCHOOL
by Stacy Towle Morgan
Join the fun as home-schoolers Hope and Annie Brown visit fascinating countries and meet inspiring Christians from around the world!

★ ★ ★

THREE COUSINS DETECTIVE CLUB®
by Elspeth Campbell Murphy
Famous detective cousins Timothy, Titus, and Sarah-Jane learn compelling Scripture-based truths while finding—and solving—intriguing mysteries.

* (ages 7–10)